*This one is for anyone who wants to read anything—bless you!*

SIMON & SCHUSTER BOOKS FOR YOUNG READERS

An imprint of Simon & Schuster Children's Publishing Division

1230 Avenue of the Americas, New York, New York 10020

Copyright © 2021 by Lydecker Publishing, Inc.

All rights reserved, including the right of reproduction in whole or in part in any form.

SIMON & SCHUSTER BOOKS FOR YOUNG READERS is a trademark of Simon & Schuster, Inc.

For information about special discounts for bulk purchases, please contact Simon & Schuster Special Sales at 1-866-506-1949 or business@simonandschuster.com.

The Simon & Schuster Speakers Bureau can bring authors to your live event. For more information or to book an event, contact the Simon & Schuster Speakers Bureau at 1-866-248-3049 or visit our website at www.simonspeakers.com.

Book design by Lucy Ruth Cummins

The text for this book was set in Grit Primer.

The illustrations for this book were rendered in ink and colored digitally.

Manufactured in China

0121 SCP

First Edition

10  9  8  7  6  5  4  3  2  1

Library of Congress Cataloging-in-Publication Data

Names: Kaplan, Bruce Eric, author, illustrator.

Title: You have to read this book! / Bruce Eric Kaplan.

Description: First edition. || New York : Simon & Schuster Books for Young Readers, [2021] || Audience: Ages 4-8. || Audience: Grades K-1. || Summary: Morris buys a book for his son, Benny, that he enjoyed as a child, but Benny stubbornly refuses to read or even listen to it—forcing Morris to ridiculous extremes, like a safari to the middle of the Sahara.

Identifiers: LCCN 2019049289 (print) || LCCN 2019049290 (ebook) || ISBN 9781534462861 (hardcover) || ISBN 9781534462878 (ebook)

Subjects: LCSH: Books and reading—Juvenile fiction. || Fathers and sons—Juvenile fiction. || Humorous stories. || CYAC: Books and reading—Fiction. || Fathers and sons—Fiction. || Humorous stories. || LCGFT: Humorous fiction. || Picture books.

Classification: LCC PZ7.K128973 Yo 2021 (print) || LCC PZ7.K128973 (ebook) || DDC 813.6 [E]—dc23

LC record available at https://lccn.loc.gov/2019049289

LC ebook record available at https://lccn.loc.gov/2019049290

SIMON & SCHUSTER BOOKS FOR YOUNG READERS

New York   London   Toronto   Sydney   New Delhi

This is the story of a very pushy father named Morris.

One day Morris was walking by a store when something caught his eye.

It was a book he had loved when he was his son Benny's age.

Morris excitedly ran into the store and bought the book.

He ran home and said,
"Benny, you have to read this book!"

Benny said, "I don't want to."

Morris curled up next to Benny and opened the book and started reading it aloud.

Benny said, "I don't like this book.
I don't need any more negative energy
in my life."

That night Morris asked Benny to pick five books for them to read before bed.

Benny picked five books, but somehow there was a sixth book at the bottom of the pile.

"No!" said Benny.

Wherever Benny went,

there was the book.

This went on for days.

Then weeks.

Then months.

One morning, Morris said,
"For breakfast, how about I make you
an ice cream sundae?

"Oh, and then we can read the book?"
he added.

Benny polished off the sundae
in three seconds, got a stomachache,
and went to bed.

"Sorry we didn't have time for the book,"
he said.

Morris started hiding Benny's books.

"Looks like this
is our only choice
tonight, little
guy," Morris said.

Benny said, "I'm tired. I'll just go to
sleep. Good night, Pop."

The next morning, Morris went to try again.

Morris searched the whole house but couldn't find Benny anywhere.

Finally, he went outside.

The sign worked.

Morris announced they were
going on vacation.

"Where?" Benny asked.

"It's a surprise."

They took a plane.

in the middle of a desert, alone,

with nothing.

Just the book.

"I don't want to read it!
I will never want to read it!"
Benny screamed.

"What kind of vacation is this?"

"I can wait," Morris said patiently.

"I want to go home," Benny wailed.
And that's when Morris realized the
camel had left.

"You really didn't think this out," Benny said.

"No, I didn't."

"Give me that book," Benny said calmly.

Morris smiled happily.
*Finally*, he thought.

Benny opened the book and looked at it. Then he ripped a page out.

"What are you doing?" Morris shrieked.

"Saving us," Benny said.
Benny took the pieces and carefully
laid them all out.

Which caught the attention of
a passing airplane and they were
miraculously rescued.

On the plane ride home, they were served rice pudding.

"This was my favorite dessert when I was a kid," Morris said. "You HAVE to try it."

"Meh," Benny said.

Morris kept pushing. They fought and fought until finally the rice pudding went SPLAT, all over Morris's face.

Morris took a lick. "This is bad. You're right. I won't make any more suggestions," he said. Then he added quietly, "At least for the rest of the plane ride."